Party Animals

PuRRmaiDS

The Scaredy Cat
The Catfish Club
Seasick Sea Horse
Search for the Mermicorn
A Star Purr-formance
Quest for Clean Water
Kittens in the Kitchen
Merry Fish-mas
Kitten Campout
A Grrr-eat New Friendship
A Purr-fect Pumpkin

MeRMicoRNs®

Sparkle Magic
A Friendship Problem
The Invisible Mix-Up
Sniffles and Surprises

PuRRmaiDS

Party Animals

by Sudipta Bardhan-Quallen

illustrations by Vivien Wu

A STEPPING STONE BOOK™
Random House 🏠 New York

Text copyright © 2022 by Sudipta Bardhan-Quallen
Cover art copyright © 2022 by Andrew Farley
Interior illustrations copyright © 2022 by Vivien Wu

All rights reserved. Published in the United States by Random House Children's Books, a division of Penguin Random House LLC, New York.

Random House and the colophon are registered trademarks and A Stepping Stone Book and the colophon are trademarks of Penguin Random House LLC. PURRMAIDS® is a registered trademark of KIKIDOODLE LLC and is used under license from KIKIDOODLE LLC.

Visit us on the Web!
rhcbooks.com

Educators and librarians, for a variety of teaching tools, visit us at
RHTeachersLibrarians.com

Library of Congress Cataloging-in-Publication Data
Names: Bardhan-Quallen, Sudipta, author. | Wu, Vivien, illustrator.
Title: Party animals / by Sudipta Bardhan-Quallen; illustrations by Vivien Wu.
Description: New York: Random House, [2022] | Series: Purrmaids; 12 |
"A Stepping Stone book" | Audience: Ages 6–9 |
Summary: "When it seems like her friends don't want to celebrate her birthday, Angel leaves the party and finds Minnie, a manatee who needs help!"
—Provided by publisher.
Identifiers: LCCN 2021042959 (print) | LCCN 2021042960 (ebook) |
ISBN 978-0-593-43308-9 (trade paperback) |
ISBN 978-0-593-43309-6 (library binding) | ISBN 978-0-593-43310-2 (ebook)
Subjects: CYAC: Birthdays—Fiction. | Schools—Fiction. | Mermaids—Fiction. |
Manatees—Fiction. | Helpfulness—Fiction. | LCGFT: Animal fiction.
Classification: LCC PZ7.B25007 Par 2022 (print) | LCC PZ7.B25007 (ebook) |
DDC [Fic]—dc23

Printed in the United States of America
10 9 8 7 6 5 4 3 2 1
First Edition

This book has been officially leveled by using
the F&P Text Level Gradient™ Leveling System.

To Snooty

1

Most of the time, the students of Room Eel-Twelve loved being at school. Their teacher, Ms. Harbor, taught paw-some lessons. The dismissal bell at the end of the day often surprised the students. They were so fin-terested in what Ms. Harbor was saying that they lost track of time.

But on a sunny afternoon in Kittentail Cove, a black-and-white kitten named Angel couldn't stop checking the clock.

She turned around again and again. After the tenth time, the orange-striped kitten next to Angel whispered, "What's going on?"

"I'm checking the time, Coral," Angel replied.

"We can all see that," whispered a kitten with silky, white fur. Her name was Shelly.

Angel frowned. "You know why!" she said. "The class always sings 'Happy Birthday' before the bell rings. We're running out of time for you all to sing to me!"

"Oh, that's right," Coral said. "It's someone's birthday today."

"Is it?" Shelly asked. But then she and Coral started to giggle. That's how Angel knew her two best friends were just squidding around.

At the front of the classroom, Ms. Harbor continued the lesson. "Many of the animals that we see in the ocean can breathe underwater. But there are some that cannot! These are called marine mammals." She floated to the board and held up her sea pen. "Can anyone name a marine mammal?"

"Seals!" Baker answered.

"And sea lions!" Taylor added.

Ms. Harbor wrote those answers on the board. "Who else can think of one?"

Umiko said, "Whales!"

Adrianna added, "Dolphins!"

"Actually," Cascade said, "dolphins are a type of whale."

Adrianna frowned.

"Cascade is right," Ms. Harbor said. "But dolphins still count!"

That made Adrianna smile again.

"Does anyone else want to name a marine mammal?" Ms. Harbor asked.

"Walruses!" Coral said.

"Otters!" Shelly added.

"Polar bears!" Angel said.

Ms. Harbor nodded at all the answers. She winked at Angel. "A lot of purrmaids don't think of polar bears as marine mammals. But they are!"

Angel grinned.

Ms. Harbor floated back and studied the board. "This is almost the whole list," she said. "But I can think of two more types of marine mammals. Does anyone know which ones?"

"Sharks?" Baker asked.

Ms. Harbor shook her head. "Sharks are fish."

"Pelicans?" Taylor asked.

"No, pelicans are birds," Ms. Harbor explained.

The students looked at each other. No one seemed to have any ideas. So Ms. Harbor went back to the board and wrote *manatees* and *dugongs* on the list.

"Of course!" Angel said. "I forgot about them!"

Marine Mammals
Seals
Walruses
Sea Lions
Otters
Whales
Polar Bears
Dolphins

"A lot of purrmaids do!" Ms. Harbor said. "You don't see manatees and dugongs as often as whales or dolphins. Many purrmaids never meet any at all. But if you do meet one, it's paw-some!"

Angel thought about another type of creature that many purrmaids don't get to meet. Those creatures were called mermicorns. They were part mermaid and part unicorn. Angel, Coral, and Shelly had two good friends named Sirena and Lily who were mermicorns. *And it really was paw-some to meet them!* Angel thought.

"Because marine mammals can't breathe underwater," Ms. Harbor continued, "they have to go back to the surface of the ocean to take breaths of air."

Coral raised her paw. "Does that mean

they are going to the surface every few seconds?"

"Not really," Ms. Harbor answered. "Some larger seals and whales can hold their breath for over an hour. Dolphins usually need to take a breath every ten minutes. Polar bears need to breathe every two minutes. Narwhals and manatees can hold their breath for around twenty minutes."

"What happens to marine mammals if they can't get to the surface?" Shelly asked.

"They could drown," Ms. Harbor said. "But don't worry. Marine mammals know to be careful. They make sure that they can get back to the surface easily." She floated to her desk and held up a textbook. "Please open your science books, everyone. I'd like you to read the chapter about marine mammals now."

"The whole chapter?" Baker asked, frowning.

"It's so long!" Taylor added.

Ms. Harbor chuckled. "You don't have to read the whole chapter. I just want you to read while I go get some supplies for our next activity."

Angel scowled. Another activity? When were they going to celebrate her birthday? Then she gasped. She leaned toward Shelly and Coral and whispered, "What if Ms. Harbor forgot my birthday?"

Coral shrugged.

Shelly said, "I don't think she would."

Angel watched Ms. Harbor swim out the classroom door. Coral put a paw on her shoulder. "Just start reading, Angel,"

Coral suggested. "Ms. Harbor will probably be back soon."

Angel sighed and opened her book. She started reading about marine mammals. She was in a bad mood, so she thought the book would be boring. But it wasn't! There were all sorts of facts about marine mammals that Angel didn't know. Like human sailors used to confuse manatees with mermaids! That made her smile. Mermaids and manatees don't look alike at all!

Angel read page after page without looking up. She was paying so much attention to the textbook that she didn't notice someone was floating next to her desk. Ms. Harbor's announcement was such a surprise that she almost jumped right out of her seat!

"All right, everyone," Ms. Harbor purred. "We are going to stop here for the day." She turned to smile at Angel. "It's time to sing to our birthday girl!"

Angel grinned. Ms. Harbor began the song. Coral and Shelly leaned closer and squeezed Angel's paws.

When the song ended, everyone clapped.

"See?" Shelly whispered. "We told you Ms. Harbor wouldn't forget your birthday!"

2

The students shouted, "Happy birthday, Angel!" Angel popped out of her seat and took a little bow.

As the dismissal bell rang, Ms. Harbor announced, "There's no homework tonight!"

That made the students cheer. Angel said, "Thank you, Ms. Harbor!"

"Is that a present for all of us?" Baker asked with a grin.

"In honor of Angel's birthday?" Taylor added.

Ms. Harbor smiled. "I hadn't thought of that," she said. "You all have been working so hard that you deserve a night off. Today being Angel's birthday is just lucky, I guess!" She patted Angel's shoulder. "I hope you have a fin-tastic day, Angel."

"I will!" Angel replied. "I'm sure Coral, Shelly, and I will think of something fun to do."

"Any birthday spent with friends is a paw-some one," Ms. Harbor said.

Angel, Shelly, and Coral swam out of the classroom. It was a bright, beautiful day outside. *Purr-fect birthday weather!* Angel thought.

As the three girls headed home, Angel said, "Since it's my birthday . . ."

"It is?" Coral asked. She and Shelly giggled again.

Angel stuck her tongue out at her friends and continued, "We have to celebrate together."

"But your party isn't tonight," Coral said.

Angel knew that. Her mother had planned a big birthday shell-ebration for Friday. But tonight, Angel was hoping to have a special party with her best friends. "We don't have to wait for the big party," she said. "Can we do something on our own?"

The other girls shrugged. But Angel didn't notice. "Do you want to come over tonight?" she continued.

"I don't know, Angel," Coral said, looking away. "We have homework."

Angel frowned. "But Ms. Harbor

just said we don't have any homework tonight!"

Coral and Shelly glanced at each other. Then Coral said, "I have to study some things."

"And I'm really tired," Shelly said. Disappointed, Angel looked down at her tail. Then Shelly added, "But maybe if Coral

finishes studying and I wake up after a nap, we can call you?"

"Maybe right before dinner?" Coral suggested.

Angel nodded. *Maybe* was better than *no. But I can't believe they want to spend my birthday resting and studying,* she thought.

The girls said goodbye in Leondra's Square. Angel went the rest of the way by herself. It wasn't a long swim. But it somehow felt longer today than usual.

Angel's mother was home when Angel got there. She was going over a list of things to do for Angel's party. There were party supplies all around. Angel saw stacks of scallop-shell plates, kelp garlands, seashell decorations, and starfish of all different colors.

When Mommy saw Angel, she put the list down and grabbed something. Then she rushed over to her daughter. "Happy birthday, Angel!" she said. "I have a small present for you to open."

"Just one?" Angel asked, taking the package.

Mommy laughed. "I'll have more for you at your party. Tomorrow."

"That's not fair!" Angel whined. "My birthday is *today*!" But she grinned and ripped open the wrapping paper. "This is a beautiful hat," she purred. It was black and white, just like Angel's fur. The brim was wide and floppy. There was a ribbon of kelp wrapped around the crown. But what Angel liked the most were the crystal letters attached to the ribbon. There was a shiny, red starfish between each of the letters—which spelled out her name!

Angel put the hat on to show Mommy. "What do you think?" she asked. The wide brim flopped over her left eye and part of her mouth. But Mommy could still see her happy smile!

"It looks fin-tastic," Mommy said, "but I don't know if anyone will recognize you. The hat is covering half your face!"

"I think it looks fancy!" Angel exclaimed. "I can't wait to show Shelly and Coral." But then her smile disappeared. She remembered something. *They're too busy for me today.*

Mommy noticed Angel's mood changing. She asked, "What's going on?"

Angel sighed. "I wanted to spend my birthday with my best friends. And I would love to show them this paw-some new hat! But Coral and Shelly decided they were too busy today." She crossed her paws over her chest. "I don't know why they don't want to be with me," she said. "I mean, it's my birthday!"

Mommy floated over to Angel. "Would you like some advice?" she asked.

"Yes, please," Angel purred.

"Whenever a purrmaid has a purr-oblem with a good friend," Mommy said, winking, "or a purr-oblem with two friends, the best thing to do is to talk it through. It's better to ask questions and hear what your friends have to say than to try to guess what they might be thinking."

Angel bit her lip. "But I think my friends don't want to talk to me!" she whined.

"Maybe that's true," Mommy said, "but you can't know for sure until you ask them." She kissed Angel's cheek. "Are you scared to talk to them?"

Angel shrugged. "I'm not afraid of talking to them," she said. Then she quietly added, "I'm scared that they'll tell me I'm right, that they don't want to be with me. And that would really hurt my feelings."

Mommy pulled Angel into a hug. "That's a really grown-up thing to under-stand," she said. "You're not a baby anymore."

"Mommy!" Angel squealed. But she hugged Mommy back.

"I don't think Shelly and Coral are going to tell you that they don't want to be with you," Mommy continued. "But I can't know for sure, either. You have to go talk to them. Hearing the truth is always better than guessing."

Angel nodded.

"So go ahead!" Mommy said. "Find your friends. See if they can talk. Just make sure you're home by dinner. I have a special meal planned for you and me!"

3

Angel put her new birthday hat into a bag. She wanted her friends to be the first purrmaids in Kittentail Cove to see it!

Soon, Angel was swimming toward Leondra's Square. She decided to go to Coral's house first. As she passed the window, she heard some voices. She peeked through the glass—and saw Coral with another purrmaid. It was Shelly!

What is Shelly doing at Coral's house?

Angel wondered. She waved at her friends. But they didn't notice. They were hunched over something on the counter and had their backs to the window. Angel could tell they were looking at it closely. Shelly pointed, and Coral nodded. Then they both laughed.

Angel frowned. Coral didn't really look like she was studying. And Shelly definitely wasn't napping. She didn't know

what they were doing. But she did know that her best friends clearly didn't want to be with her on her birthday.

Angel didn't want Shelly and Coral to see that she was there. She floated down to the floor and out of sight. She didn't really know what to do next.

Mommy said she should talk things out with her friends. *But how am I supposed to talk to them about this?* Angel

thought. *They made up a story so they wouldn't have to spend the afternoon with me. And it's my birthday!*

Angel was trying to decide if she wanted to talk to her friends when she heard Coral's front door opening. She ducked behind a large kelp bush. Shelly and Coral swam past. They were so busy talking that they didn't even look in Angel's direction.

"I'm so glad we convinced Angel to go home after school," Coral purred.

"This will be so much easier without her," Shelly agreed.

Angel gulped. *I never knew they wanted to get rid of me,* she thought. She felt tears welling in her eyes.

Then Coral said, "This is going to be so much fun!"

"I know!" Shelly exclaimed. "I wish

we had thought about doing this a long time ago!"

As the purrmaids swam farther away, Angel realized she wasn't just feeling sad. She was also feeling a little angry. *If they don't like something about me,* she thought, *why don't they just tell me?* Angel never meant to be annoying. But it wasn't very friendly for Coral and Shelly to make up a story just to get away from her!

Angel clenched her paws. She was going to find out what was so important to Shelly and Coral that they would treat her like this. *I'm going to follow them,* she thought.

Angel popped out from behind the kelp. She didn't want her friends to know that she was there. Suddenly, she had an idea! She took her birthday hat out of her bag. She remembered what Mommy had said about the hat hiding her face. Maybe that would be useful.

Soon, Angel was following her friends through Kittentail Cove. They stopped at the Lake Restaurant. They swam in for a few minutes. When they left, they were carrying a box.

"That's probably a picnic," Angel muttered.

"Let's hurry," she heard Shelly say. "We need to get to the South Canary Current. It's probably already really crowded."

Coral nodded. "I'm sure two little purrmaids will be able to fit," she replied.

Angel clenched her paws again. *I guess three purrmaids would have been too many,* she thought. *But they're wrong. I am going to find out the truth about today, no matter what!*

4

There were a lot of purrmaids waiting to ride the South Canary Current. Angel wanted to keep an eye on Coral and Shelly. She pushed her way closer to them. But Angel went a little too far! Shelly accidentally floated backward and bumped into Angel! Shelly looked over her shoulder and said, "Excuse me!"

Oh no, Angel thought. She was certain that Shelly would recognize her right away. But Shelly only smiled and turned back to Coral. *My birthday hat is like a disguise!* Angel thought.

It was good that the hat covered most of Angel's face. It kept her friends from knowing she was there. And it also kept anyone from seeing how hurt she was.

When it was time to ride the current, Angel made sure she wasn't too close to the other girls. They got off at the stop for Tortoiseshell Reef, and Angel quietly followed. She pulled the hat down to hide more of her face so her friends wouldn't know it was her. *Let's see what Coral and Shelly are up to!* Angel thought. There were butterfly fish fluttering in her tummy. She wanted to know, but she also didn't want to know.

Usually, Angel and her friends would swim through Tortoiseshell Reef slowly. They would stop to see the beautiful creatures, seashells, and corals that were all around. They would even clean up any trash that had floated down and settled on the reef. But today, Coral and Shelly were moving very quickly. They weren't paying attention to anything else. That made it easy for Angel to follow them.

Shelly and Coral raced right toward Ponyfish Grotto. Angel remembered the hidden spot that Sirena had shown them. There was a rock-and-coral tunnel that led to a large cave. She guessed that her friends would be headed to the secret entrance.

The two girls stopped for a moment

to look for something. Angel crouched behind an elkhorn coral and watched them. Suddenly, they disappeared!

I know about the secret cave, too. Why didn't Shelly and Coral invite me? Angel wondered. She was still angry. But she was hurt, too. She squeezed her eyes shut to keep the tears from falling.

Then Angel made a decision. *I'm going to go ask them why,* she thought. She floated out from behind the elkhorn. She tried to get up the courage to follow her friends into the cave.

But something stopped her.

Just when Angel was ready to swim to the tunnel, someone else appeared. Actually, two someones. They both had mermaid tails. But the other half of these someones were unicorns. Angel recognized the rainbow mane and the pink-and-purple mane immediately. It was Sirena and Lily!

All of a sudden, Angel realized something. *All four of my friends wanted to see each other,* she thought. She gulped. *But none of them wanted to see me!*

Angel felt like she was frozen inside

an iceberg. At the same time, her face felt hot enough to boil the ocean. She wanted to leave right away. She wanted to get as far as she could so no one would see her crying.

But then Angel heard someone neigh, "Is that a purrmaid?"

Someone else replied, "I think so. But I can't see who it is. That fancy hat is in the way!"

Angel turned toward the sounds. The voices belonged to Lily and Sirena. Lily shouted, "Angel, is that you?"

But Angel didn't answer. She spun around and swam away as quickly as she could. She didn't even notice that her hat fell off because she was moving so fast. *My friends don't want to be with me,* she thought. *So I don't want to be with them, either!*

5

Angel didn't stop swimming for a long time. She couldn't really see where she was going—there were too many tears in her eyes. She just knew she had to get away. She headed for the coral tunnel at the edge of Tortoiseshell Reef. She squeezed through the small opening, and she slowed down when she reached a patch of open water.

That's when Angel realized she had

dropped something. "My birthday hat!" she exclaimed. She hadn't thought her birthday could get any worse than finding out all her friends didn't like her. But now she'd lost Mommy's birthday present! *I wish I hadn't followed my friends,* Angel thought.

There were a few rocks on the sandy ocean floor. One rock caught Angel's eye. It was the biggest one. But the more finteresting thing was that there seemed to be a string of sea-glass beads hanging off a part of the rock. The sea glass twinkled when beams of sunlight filtered down from the surface of the water.

Angel floated over to the rock. She slumped against it and took a deep breath. Even though she was all alone, she didn't want to cry anymore. It was still her birthday. No one should cry on their birthday.

"This is the worst birthday ever," Angel muttered.

Suddenly, Angel heard a voice. It said, "Why is it the worst birthday?"

The voice was coming from the rock she was sitting on!

Angel quickly popped up. Her mouth fell open. *Rocks don't talk!* she thought. She wondered if she had imagined the voice.

But then Angel heard another question. "Did you hear what I said?"

This isn't a rock! Angel thought. "Hello?" she said. "Is anybody there?"

"I'm right here!" the rock replied. "You were just sitting on me."

Angel swam a little closer. She needed to get a better look.

The rock began to slowly turn around. *Very* slowly. When it finally stopped turning, Angel saw that the rock wasn't a rock at all. "You're a manatee!" Angel cried.

"I am!" the manatee said. "My name is Minnie. And you smushed me!"

"I'm so sorry!" Angel said. "I thought you were a rock."

Minnie grinned. "That happens to manatees a lot."

Angel realized that the sea-glass beads she thought were stuck to the rock were actually a necklace around Minnie's neck. "Your necklace is very purr-ty," she said.

"Thank you!" Minnie answered.

The girls smiled at each other. "I've never met a manatee before," Angel said.

Minnie winked. "Well, I've never met a purrmaid before!"

"Why are you out here alone?" Angel asked.

"I didn't start alone," Minnie said, shrugging. "I was out for a swim with my friends, Dolly and Celia."

Angel scratched her head. "Are they manatees, too?"

Minnie said, "No, Dolly is a dolphin, and Celia is a seal. They swim a lot faster than I do. Usually, they wait for me. But they didn't feel like it today."

"I know what it's like when your friends decide they could have more fun without you," Angel purred. "That's what happened to me."

"I don't think they decided they could have more fun without me," Minnie said. "I've talked to them about this. Sometimes they want to swim fast, and I want to swim slowly." She smiled. "Or not swim at all! But even when we're apart, we are always friends."

Angel looked down at her tail. "Maybe your friends do something different. But I don't think that's what happened with my friends."

"Have you talked to them?" Minnie asked.

Angel shook her head.

"Maybe you should," Minnie said. "There might be something else going on that you don't know about."

Angel bit her lip. Mommy had said the same thing.

"Besides," Minnie continued, "sometimes, being alone can feel bad. But other times, it can be fun! You could have an adventure you never expected. Like meeting a manatee!"

"You might be right," Angel agreed. "I wouldn't have gone past the edge of Tortoiseshell Reef if I'd been with my friends."

"See?" Minnie said. "You probably had a misunderstanding. But it turned out to be lucky!"

Angel sighed. "I still don't think it was a misunderstanding. And it really hurts today because it's my birthday."

"That's right—it's your birthday!" Minnie exclaimed. "I love birthdays! And birthday parties, and birthday games, and birthday songs—"

"My class sang to me at sea school," Angel said. "But no one is singing now."

"We can fix that!" Minnie said. She took a bow and then began to sing.

Your birthday is a special day,
a day to laugh and cheer!
Everyone's been waiting for your
birthday to be here.
I hope the day is filled with every
good thing in the sea.
I'm so happy that I am your
birthday manatee!

6

Minnie finished the song by spinning around in the water. A million bubbles surrounded them both.

"That was paw-some!" Angel said, clapping and giggling. The bubbles tickled!

The manatee took another bow.

"I've never heard that birthday song before," Angel said.

"You've never had a birthday manatee

to celebrate with before!" Minnie said. But as she was talking, Minnie began to float upward.

Angel thought, *She can't be leaving!* "Where are you going?" she asked.

"I need to get to the surface of the water," Minnie replied. "I have to go take a breath."

"Of course!" Angel exclaimed, following the manatee up. "Marine mammals can't breathe underwater!"

"How did you know that?" Minnie asked.

Angel grinned. "We learned about you in school today. We also learned that purrmaids don't really see manatees near Kittentail Cove. I can't wait to tell Shelly, Coral, Sirena, and Lily about meeting you." But then Angel stopped swimming. She remembered that her friends didn't want to see her.

Angel sighed. She couldn't spend the whole afternoon being sad about her friends. She caught up to Minnie and floated next to her at the surface.

Minnie took a breath. "Wow," she said. "Today started out as such a beautiful day. Now look."

The sky wasn't
bright and sunny
anymore. It was
filled with dark,
angry clouds. Angel
thought the sky looked
the way she felt.

But then Angel noticed
something. A small flicker
of sunlight peeked through the
clouds, right over Minnie's head.

Angel realized that maybe the storm
clouds and the sunlight were a lot like this
birthday. Maybe making a new friend was
a ray of sunshine on a dark, cloudy day.

"Take a deep breath, Minnie!" Angel
shouted.

Minnie looked puzzled. "I always do,"
she replied. "But why?"

Angel waved for Minnie to follow. "I

have a fin-tastic idea," she said. "Let me take you back to Kittentail Cove. We can have our own paw-some birthday celebration, just the two of us!"

"Not so fast," Minnie said.

Angel froze. Was Minnie going to say no to her plan? "We could stay here instead," she said quietly.

Minnie shook her head. "Actually, going to Kittentail Cove sounds like a manatee-rrific plan."

"Then why did you stop me?" Angel asked.

Minnie grinned. "I didn't stop you! I just said not to go so fast. Manatees have to take it easy!"

Both girls giggled. "This way!" Angel called.

The two new friends swam back toward Tortoiseshell Reef. Angel told

Minnie all about Kittentail Cove. "I'll take you everywhere," she told Minnie. "My mother probably has a cake ready for me, and we can share that. It doesn't matter if there's no one else there, either."

"I do love birthday cake," Minnie said. "And maybe I could help you speak to your friends. In case there really was a misunderstanding."

Angel frowned. She turned her face away so Minnie couldn't see. "Maybe we could do that," she mumbled.

After they had been swimming for a while, Minnie asked, "Is it much farther to Kittentail Cove?"

Angel squinted to see into the distance. She could just make out the rocks at the edge of Tortoiseshell Reef. "Not too far," she purred, pointing.

But then Angel saw something else.

Four figures were swimming toward the coral tunnel, too. She spied flashes of orange, white, pink, and rainbow. *It's Coral, Shelly, Lily, and Sirena!* Angel realized. *I'm not ready to talk to them yet. I'm still too hurt.*

"Maybe we should take a little break," Angel suggested.

"You don't have to ask a manatee twice!" Minnie answered. She drifted down to the ocean floor and sat very still. She looked like a giant rock, like before. "Just a few minutes," she said. She closed her eyes.

Angel joined Minnie down on the sand. But she made sure Minnie would block her friends' view if they looked over in their direction.

Hiding from Lily, Sirena, Coral, and Shelly wasn't the bravest thing to do. Angel knew that. Usually, she was much braver—but, usually, she had her friends to help her be brave. How was she supposed to find courage when she didn't have her friends on her side?

7

Angel's mind was racing as she crouched behind Minnie. *It's hard to be brave alone,* she thought. *But I'm not really alone—I have Minnie.* Minnie had already offered to help Angel talk to the other girls.

Angel realized she could try to be brave with Minnie's help. She peeked out over Minnie's head to find her friends again. But they had disappeared!

"I'm too late!" Angel said, sighing.

"Have I been resting for too long?" Minnie asked, startled.

Angel shook her head. "No, not at all. I was just thinking about something else."

Minnie smiled. "We can get going now."

Angel stared at the spot her friends had been. *They probably went back through the tunnel,* she thought. Maybe she could still catch them if she was fast.

But before she could tell Minnie to hurry, the manatee said, "I'll go take another quick breath." She started to float up to the surface again.

"We're almost there," Angel said, frowning. "Why don't you wait until we've crossed over into Tortoiseshell Reef?"

"It's probably better to do it now,"

Minnie replied. "I get worried about not being able to breathe."

Angel shrugged. "That's fine." It was probably too late to catch the other girls, anyway.

Once Minnie had taken a deep breath, Angel asked, "Ready now?"

Minnie nodded, so they raced deeper into the ocean together. Or, at least, Angel tried to race! Minnie kept reminding her, "Manatees have to take their time!"

Angel always hated waiting. And right then, every minute they wasted was another minute her friends spent swimming away! But Minnie didn't know that. Angel decided she would have to be more patient. "I'm sorry, Minnie," she purred. "I'm just so excited to show you Kitten-tail Cove!"

"And I appreciate that," Minnie said. "I'm sorry I'm so slow."

"It's not your fault," Angel said, shaking her head. She didn't want Minnie to feel bad about anything. So she forced herself to slow down. "I'm not being very patient. I'll try to do better." *It's worth it,* she thought. *This can still be a special birthday with a friend. Thanks to Minnie!*

It took a little longer than Angel wanted, but she finally led Minnie to the coral tunnel. "Kittentail Cove is on the other side," she explained.

"Exciting!" Minnie exclaimed.

Angel agreed. But then she looked carefully at the opening of the tunnel and then at Minnie. She scratched her head. "Are you going to fit inside that?" she asked.

Minnie floated to the opening and slowly poked her head into the tunnel. She inched forward until she was halfway in. Then she spun around like she had after her birthday song. The water filled with a million bubbles again. Minnie shouted, "It's just big enough!"

Angel grinned. "What are we waiting for?"

Angel darted through the tunnel. When she got to the other side, she turned around and said, "Come on, Minnie!"

Minnie moved through the tunnel. "Almost there!" she said, smiling.

But as Angel watched, Minnie's smile turned upside down. She also stopped moving closer.

"Is something wrong, Minnie?" Angel asked.

Minnie's head was sticking out of the coral tunnel. But the rest of her body was stuffed inside. "Angel," she wailed, "I'm stuck!"

8

Angel floated closer to Minnie. "What do you mean?" she asked.

Minnie tried to wiggle around. But she couldn't. "This tunnel is smaller than I thought!" Minnie cried. "I can't get through to you."

Angel took a careful look at the tunnel. There was a rock jammed into the coral. It made the opening on the Tortoiseshell Reef side a little smaller. "This rock is in your way," Angel said. She grabbed it and tried to pull it away. But it was too heavy!

Angel scowled. "Can you go backward and out the other side?"

Minnie started to cry. "Manatees can't swim backward!" she said. "And there's not enough room for me to turn around." She sniffled. "It's a good thing I took a breath before I tried to get through the tunnel. I'm all right for now, but I can't stay here forever. I need to get to the surface soon."

Angel's eyes grew wide. She tried to remember what Ms. Harbor had said about manatees. *I think they can hold their breath for twenty minutes.* That gave her a little bit of time.

"I got you into this," Angel said, "and

I'm going to get you out, too. Try not to worry!"

Minnie gulped. "What are you going to do?"

Angel knew she had to get help from someone. She *could* go all the way home and get Mommy. She'd know what to do. But it would take too long to get there and back. Minnie wouldn't be able to hold her breath that long.

That's not going to work, Angel thought. All the adults in town were too far away. But Angel's friends were much closer.

Angel didn't want to talk to Coral, Shelly, Sirena, or Lily. Her feelings were still hurt. *They made it clear they don't want me around,* she thought. It would be so embarrassing to ask them for help.

But then Angel thought about Minnie.

She was in real trouble. Helping her was the most important thing.

"Hold on, Minnie," Angel said. She straightened up and floated tall. She hoped that made her look confident. "I'm going to find help! I'll be right back, I purr-omise!"

"Please go fast!" Minnie replied.

❀ ❀ ❀

Angel followed Minnie's fin-structions. She swam as fast as she could. She went straight to Ponyfish Grotto. She didn't have to go as far as the secret tunnel to find her friends, though. They were all outside. They saw her coming—and they weren't smiling.

"Angel!" Shelly said. "What are you doing here?"

Angel took a deep breath. "I know you guys don't want to be around me," she said, "but I need your help!"

"What do you mean, we don't want to be around you?" Lily asked.

"We've been out looking for you," Sirena added. "But we couldn't find you anywhere."

Angel frowned. "You've been looking for me? How did you even know I was here?"

"I thought I saw you outside," Lily neighed. "But when I called your name, you swam away."

"I was sure that Lily was imagining it," Sirena said.

Shelly held something out. "But then Lily and Sirena found this," she said.

"And we guessed it belonged to you," Coral said.

Angel stared down at Shelly's paws. "My birthday hat!" she exclaimed. In all the excitement with Minnie, she had completely forgotten that she had lost it.

Lily held out a bag with six red starfish in it. "I think these fell off when you dropped the hat. We gathered them in case you wanted to fix it later."

"We hurried up with our surprise," Shelly purred, "so we could go find you."

Angel bit her lip. What did her friends mean by *surprise*? But then she remembered why she was there. "There's no time for a surprise!" she cried. "My friend Minnie is in trouble! You all have to come with me. We have to get moving!"

Right away, everyone answered, "Let's go!"

Angel led her friends toward the edge of Tortoiseshell Reef. She explained while they swam. "Minnie is a manatee," she said.

"A manatee!" Coral replied. "I've never met a manatee!"

"Me neither," Shelly, Sirena, and Lily said together.

"That's not what's important right now," Angel said. "Minnie is stuck in the tunnel that leads into Tortoiseshell Reef. There's a very heavy rock in the way. I can't move it by myself." She frowned. "If Minnie can't get free, she can't swim to the surface."

"And she can't take another breath!" Shelly exclaimed.

"That's why I need all of you to help me!" Angel said.

"Don't worry, Angel," Sirena said. "We'll get your friend free!"

9

Angel could finally see Minnie up ahead. She was still wedged into the tunnel. She looked scared.

"Angel!" Minnie shouted. "You're back!"

"And she brought friends!" Lily neighed.

"I'll introduce you all later," Angel said. She floated closer to the rock that was in Minnie's way. "Help me move this!"

Together, the three purrmaids and the two mermicorns grabbed the rock. "On the count of three, we'll all lift," Angel said.

The other girls nodded.

"One," Angel said. "Two. THREE!"

The girls pulled with all their might. The rock didn't move.

Angel scratched her head. Then she had an idea. "While we try to lift the rock again, I need you to do something, Minnie."

"What?" Minnie asked.

"Remember the spin from the end of the birthday song?" Angel asked.

"Yes," Minnie answered.

"I want you to do that," Angel said.

"I think the bubbles would help get you free."

"I can try," Minnie said. "But I'm really, really stuck!"

Angel turned to the other girls. "I'll count to three again, all right?"

When Angel got to three, the girls lifted—but the rock barely moved.

"Keep lifting!" Angel shouted.

"Please do your best!" Minnie cried.

The rock wiggled just a little bit.

"We've loosened it!" Coral said.

"Don't stop now!" Shelly added.

Angel flicked her tail and pulled up on the rock as hard as she could. So did the other girls. The wiggle got bigger and bigger. And then Minnie started to rock back and forth. All of a sudden, a burst of bubbles filled the water. Angel, Coral,

Shelly, Sirena, and Lily all went tumbling backward.

The rock was free—and so was Minnie!

"Oof!" Angel yelped from the ocean floor. The rock sunk down and rested on the sand next to her.

Angel looked around. Lily and Coral were on the ocean floor, too. Sirena and Shelly were brushing sand out of their hair. "But where's Minnie?" she asked.

Sirena pointed. "There!" Minnie was swimming to the surface of the ocean as quickly as she could.

"That's the fastest moving manatee I've ever seen," Coral said.

"You've never seen a manatee up close before," Shelly said.

The girls giggled. Angel popped up off the sand. She grinned. "Let's see if we can catch her!"

Minnie reached the surface first. She took a few deep breaths before Angel caught up to her. "You did it, Angel!" she gasped. "You saved me!"

"I couldn't have done it alone," Angel said. She turned to Coral, Shelly, Sirena, and Lily. "I know you had other things you wanted to do today. Thank you for helping me." She looked down at her tail. "I won't bother you anymore."

"Angel," Coral purred, "you're not bothering us!"

"You're our friend," Shelly added.

Angel frowned. "Some friends!" she shouted. "You tried to get away from me. And you met up together in secret, without me." She couldn't hold her tears back any longer. She looked down at her tail so the others wouldn't see. "You didn't want to be with me on my birthday. You changed your mind only because you knew I'd seen you."

"Is that what you think?" Lily asked, floating forward.

Angel shrugged without looking up.

"Oh, Angel," Sirena neighed. "You've got it all wrong."

"You're only saying that now," Angel said, sniffling. "I know what's really going on."

Minnie floated up to face Angel. "Angel," she said, "I don't know any of you very well. But it sure does look like you misunderstood what your friends were doing." She smiled. "They all came right away when you asked them to help me. That doesn't sound like they don't care about you."

"Come with us," Coral said. She took Angel's paw. "We want to show you something."

"Not so fast," Minnie said.

Everyone turned to look at Minnie. "I thought you wanted me to give my friends a chance," Angel said.

Minnie giggled. "I do want that. It's just that you guys can't swim so fast. Manatees have to take it easy!"

10

The girls made their way back to the secret cave. They all decided that they wouldn't make Minnie squeeze through another tunnel. Instead, they blindfolded Angel and asked her to wait in the clearing outside. "Minnie," Shelly said, "can you make sure Angel stays still?"

Minnie grinned. "I'll stay still with her to make sure!"

It felt like Angel had to wait fur-ever.

She kept asking Minnie if the others were back yet. Minnie laughed every time and said, "Just be patient!"

The tenth time Angel asked, Minnie didn't answer. "Minnie?" Angel said. "Are you still there?"

Then Angel felt paws untying the blindfold. "Take a look," Coral said.

Angel did just that. And she could hardly believe her eyes! Her friends were all smiling and wearing birthday hats. There were birthday decorations all over the clearing.

Sirena pointed to a pearl garland that was strung along the corals. "I have an oyster garden at home," she said. "Lily and I gathered the pearls to make this."

Shelly floated toward Angel with a tray. "Coral and I made this birthday cake for you," she said.

"Well, Shelly made most of the cake," Coral said. "I made sure she followed the recipe!"

"This is what you picked up at the Lake Restaurant!" Angel said.

Coral nodded. "We only told you we were busy this afternoon so we could set up a surprise for you."

Angel looked down at her tail. "I thought you didn't want to hang out with me. And then, when I saw Sirena and Lily, I thought all four of you didn't like me anymore."

"How could we ever stop liking you, Angel?" Lily neighed. She floated up to hug Angel. It quickly turned into a group hug when everyone joined in. Everyone except Minnie.

Angel frowned. "Is everything all right, Minnie?" she asked.

Minnie shrugged. "Yes, of course. I just wanted to give you and your friends some space."

"But you're our friend, too!" Angel said. All the other girls nodded. "Come join us!"

Minnie grinned. "Not so fast," she replied. But when she winked, Angel knew what to say next.

"Manatees need to take it slow!" Angel said, laughing.

❧ ❧ ❧

All together, the six new friends had a celebration. Minnie taught them the manatee birthday song. Then they each had a piece of birthday cake.

It was almost time to go home. Lily and Sirena told Minnie they could swim together. "At least, part of the way," Sirena said.

"You will be able to get home from here, right, Minnie?" Lily asked.

Minnie giggled. "The tunnel is manatee-sized now," she said, "so I'll be able to get home. Slowly!"

"Will you come to see me again?" Angel asked.

"I hope so!" Minnie answered. "It's been nice to meet all of you. I've never had purrmaid or mermicorn friends before."

"And you're our first manatee friend!" Shelly said.

"We should get going now," Coral said.

Angel nodded. She had to get back in time for a special dinner with Mommy. But it still made her sad that everyone had to leave. It had been a birthday filled with surprises. She never wanted to forget it.

Then Angel remembered something. "The starfish!" she said. She took the bag out and poured the starfish into her palm. Then she handed one to each of her friends.

"What is this?" Shelly asked.

"Instead of gluing these onto my hat," Angel said, "I want to give a starfish to

each of you. I'm going to put mine on my bracelet."

"I'll do that, too!" Coral exclaimed.

"Me too," Shelly added.

"Sirena and I can put our starfish on our pearl necklaces," Lily said.

"And I can put it on my sea-glass necklace," Minnie said.

Angel grinned. "Every time we see them, they'll remind us of today. The day I made a new friend by accident. And the day I found out that *all* my friends are the best friends in the whole entire ocean!"

The purrmaids have lots of friends around the ocean!

Read on for a sneak peek!

Early one morning in Seadragon Bay, a young mermicorn named Sirena could not sleep. She pushed the curtain on her window open. It was still dark outside! No one in the Cheval family would be awake yet.

Sirena fluffed her pillow. She pulled the blanket over her head. But she kept tossing and turning. *I'm too excited to sleep,* she thought. *What if today is the day?*

It was the first day of the season. For most mermicorns, that was just another day. But for all the colts and fillies in Seadragon Bay, it was special. That was when the Mermicorn Magic Academy invited new students to the school.

Magic was a part of mermicorn life. But like everything else, magic had to be learned. The best place for that was the Magic Academy. "I hope they pick me today!" Sirena whispered to herself. She finally gave up on sleeping. She floated out of bed and started to get dressed.

Sirena found her lucky blue top and put it on. She brushed out her long rainbow mane. She put on her favorite crystal earrings. Then she peeked out the window again. She could see some sunlight. *It's early,* she thought, *but maybe the mail is already here?*

Sirena swam toward the front door. She tried to be as quiet as a jellyfish. She didn't want to wake her family. But when she passed the kitchen, she saw that her parents were already up!

"Why are you awake?" Sirena asked.

Mom laughed. "Is that how you say good morning?"

Sirena sighed. "I'm sorry," she said. "I just wasn't expecting you. It's so early!" She swam to her parents and kissed their cheeks. "Good morning, Mom. Good morning, Dad."

"Good morning, Sirena," Dad neighed. "Are you hungry?"

Sirena nodded.

Dad started to put kelp pancakes on a plate. Mom floated over to Sirena. "So," Mom said, "today could be the day, right?"

Sirena nodded.

"That's why we're awake," Dad said.

"The day a colt or filly gets invited to join the Mermicorn Magic Academy is a big deal for parents," Mom added.

"I think a special day calls for a special breakfast," Dad said. His horn began to twinkle.